W9-BSG-654

Disney's

THE LION KING

Adapted by Margo Hover

Drawn by Judy Barnes
Painted by Robbin Cuddy

A GOLDEN BOOK • NEW YORK

Western Publishing Company, Inc., Racine, Wisconsin 53404

© 1994 The Walt Disney Company. All rights reserved. Printed in the U.S.A. No part of this book may be reproduced or copied in any form without written permission from the copyright owner. GOLDEN, GOLDEN & DESIGN, GOLDENCRAFT, A GOLDEN BOOK, A GOLDEN LOOK-LOOK BOOK, and A GOLDEN LOOK-LOOK BOOK & DESIGN are registered trademarks of Western Publishing Company, Inc. Library of Congress Catalog Card Number: 93-80334 ISBN: 0-307-12792-3/ISBN: 0-307-62792-6 (lib. bdg.) MCMXCIV

It was a day of rejoicing on the African plain. A throng of animals had gathered to witness a great event—the presentation of the first cub born to Mufasa, the Lion King, and his queen, Sarabi.

An old and wise baboon named Rafiki led the ceremony. Rafiki, the mystic of the Pride Lands, stood on Pride Rock and held the cub high for all to see.

The animals below were filled with joy. The little creature held so high was the Pride Lands' future king.

Afterward Mufasa went to look for his younger brother Scar. When Mufasa found him, Scar was teasing Zazu, the hornbill who was the king's chief minister of affairs.

"Scar, stop it!" said Mufasa. Then he asked his brother why he hadn't been at the presentation.

Scar replied angrily that if Simba had not been born, he, Scar, would be next in line to be king. Then he turned and walked away.

In time the cub, named Simba, grew strong. One day he stood on Pride Rock as his father showed him the kingdom that would one day be his. "What about that shadowy place?" asked Simba.

"It's beyond our borders," said Mufasa. "Never go there." Then he told his son how important it was to be a good king, one who understood that every creature had a place in the Circle of Life.

Later that day, before Zazu could prevent it, Simba talked his
best friend, Nala, into an adventure. They would go just beyond the
northern border—to the very place that Simba's father had said he
must never go.

"Uncle Scar told me about an elephant graveyard there!" said
Simba excitedly as he and Nala raced along side by side.

When Simba and Nala reached the graveyard, three hungry
hyenas appeared. They had been sent by Scar to hunt down Simba.
"There he is," said Shenzi, the leader. "A king fit for a meal."
The cubs managed to escape from the hyenas, only to find
themselves trapped in an elephant carcass. Suddenly the Lion King
himself appeared. He let out a huge roar, and the hyenas fled.

The angry king sent Nala home with Zazu. As night fell, he and Simba had a talk.

Simba said he was sorry that he had disobeyed his father. "I was just trying to be brave," he said.

"Being brave doesn't mean going to look for trouble," said his father. Then Mufasa explained that the great kings of the past looked down from the starry sky, ready to guide Simba.

Later Scar met with the hyenas. He was furious that they let the cubs get away.

"They weren't exactly alone," said Shenzi. "What were we supposed to do, kill Mufasa?"

"Precisely," said Scar. Then he told the hyenas there were going to be some changes. "Mufasa and his son will both die," he said. "Then I will be king and you will control the Pride Lands!"

The next day Scar lured Simba into a deep gorge, then secretly signaled the hyenas to start a stampede of wildebeests. Mufasa came and dragged Simba to safety, but the king was pulled back down by the stampede.

As Mufasa struggled to escape a second time, he called out, "Scar, help me."

"Long live the king," answered Scar, pushing his brother to his death below.

The king was dead. When Simba found out, he thought his father's death was his fault. Scar told him there was only one thing to do: "Run, Simba. Run away."

Scar then ordered the hyenas to chase and kill Simba, but the cub escaped through a thorn patch.

"If you ever come back, we'll kill you!" the hyenas screamed as the terrified cub fled into the jungle.

Scar climbed Pride Rock and announced that both Mufasa and his son were dead. He pronounced himself king and ushered the hyenas into the Pride Lands.

Simba ran and ran until he fell from exhaustion. Fortunately, he
was rescued by two friends—a clever meerkat named Timon and a
well-padded warthog named Pumbaa. Pumbaa wanted to help the
young lion. "He's just a cub," Pumbaa said. "Can we keep him?"

"Are you nuts?" Timon squealed. "Lions eat guys like us!"

In the end, Timon took pity on Simba, and he and Pumbaa
dragged the cub into the shade of the jungle.

Although Simba was soon healthy again, he could not forget his last terrible day in the Pride Lands. Timon and Pumbaa tried to teach him about *hakuna matata*, life without worry.

"No past, no future, no problems, live for today!" Timon urged.

Slowly Simba agreed that putting the past behind him was the answer. And so Simba grew up in his new friends' never-never land.

One day Simba came to Pumbaa's rescue when the poor warthog was attacked by a lioness. As Simba fought off the lioness, he suddenly realized she was Nala, his childhood friend.

"Everyone thinks you're dead," said Nala when she recognized Simba. "I've really missed you."

"I've missed you, too," said Simba. As he gazed at Nala, Simba noticed that they had both grown up.

Later Nala told Simba about life in the Pride Lands with Scar as king. "There is no food or water," she explained. "If you don't do something, everyone will starve!"

"I can't go back," Simba said. "There's nothing I can do about it. So why worry?"

"Because it's your responsibility!" Nala told him.
But Simba still believed he had caused his father's death.
He could never show his face in the Pride Lands again.

As if by magic, wise old Rafiki appeared that moonlit night and led Simba into the jungle.

Suddenly Simba heard his father's voice. As Simba gazed up at the star-filled sky, the Lion King said, "You are my son and the one true king. Now you must take your place in the Circle of Life."

The vision in the stars began to fade. "Don't leave me!" Simba cried. "Father . . ."

But Mufasa's image was gone, and Simba knew that his father was right. Simba was ready to return to his kingdom.

Before dawn the next day, Nala awakened Timon and Pumbaa and told them that she could not find Simba.

A strange voice suddenly spoke from a nearby tree. "You won't find him here," said Rafiki. "The king has returned!" As soon as he had spoken, the baboon mysteriously disappeared.

Nala realized that Simba had gone back to challenge Scar. Her heart told her to follow Simba home to the Pride Lands.

It was dusk when Simba saw Pride Rock once again. The land around it was parched and dusty.

At the very moment that Simba approached, Scar was in a rage. Many animal herds had long since left the land, and there was nothing left for the lionesses to hunt. In his terrible anger, Scar struck and stunned Sarabi, Simba's mother.

Moments later Simba confronted Scar. "Either step down or fight!" he commanded.

But Scar wasn't ready to step down. He backed the true Lion King toward the edge of the rock. Simba's back paws slipped, but he caught the edge with his front claws. Thinking that Simba could not hold on, Scar said, "This was just the way your father looked before he died—that is, before I killed him."

"Murderer!" Simba screamed, leaping up at Scar.
Simba chased his uncle until Scar begged for mercy.
But just as Simba was ready to let him go, Scar lunged
at him. As they fought, Simba's wretched uncle fell
to the ground below. Scar's terrible rule was over.
Soon a healing rain began to fall. As his mother
and friends watched, Simba claimed his kingdom.

Peace returned to the Pride Lands, and the Circle of Life continued when a cub was born to Nala and Simba, the true Lion King.

On the day of the presentation at Pride Rock, Rafiki lifted the cub high for all to see. He was the Pride Lands' future king.